Fantastic Skulls
Adult Coloring Book

ISBN 9798363494802

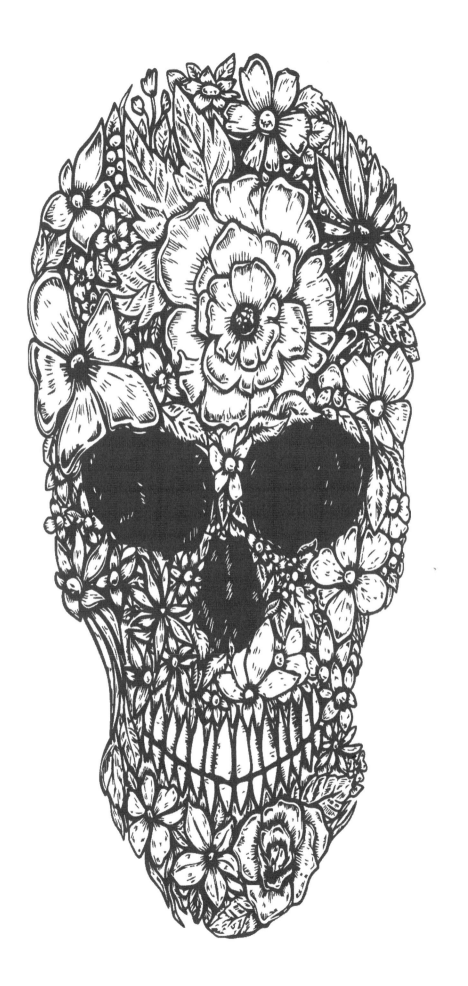

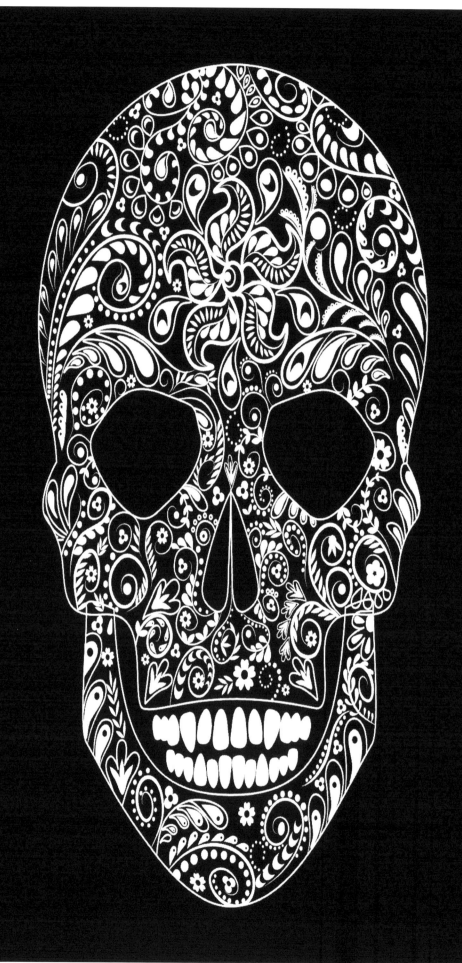

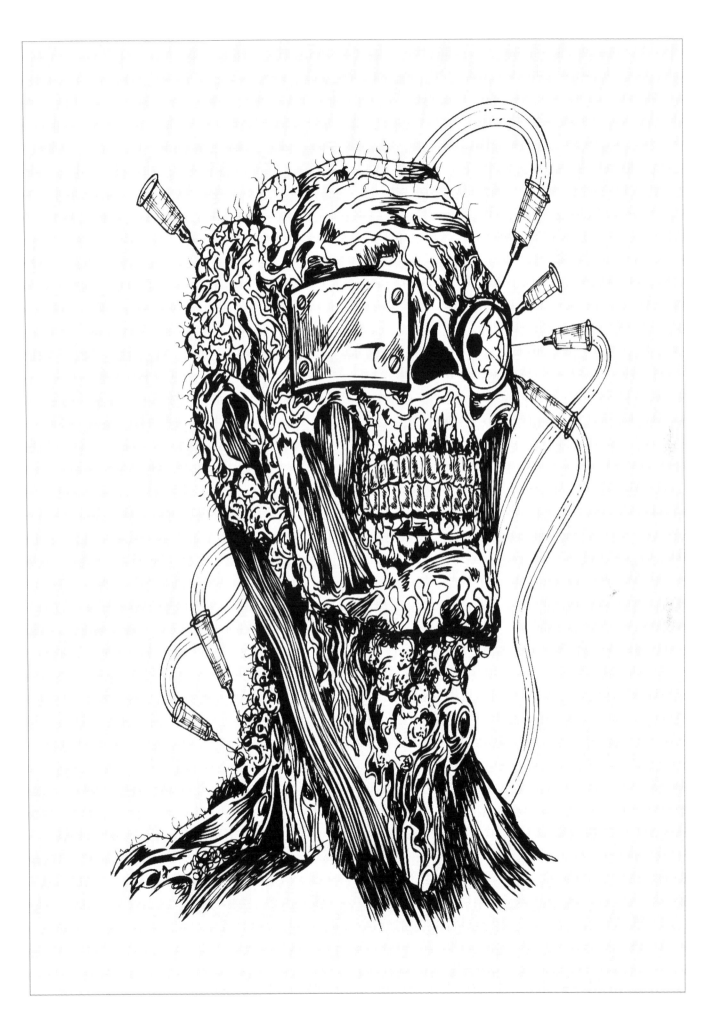

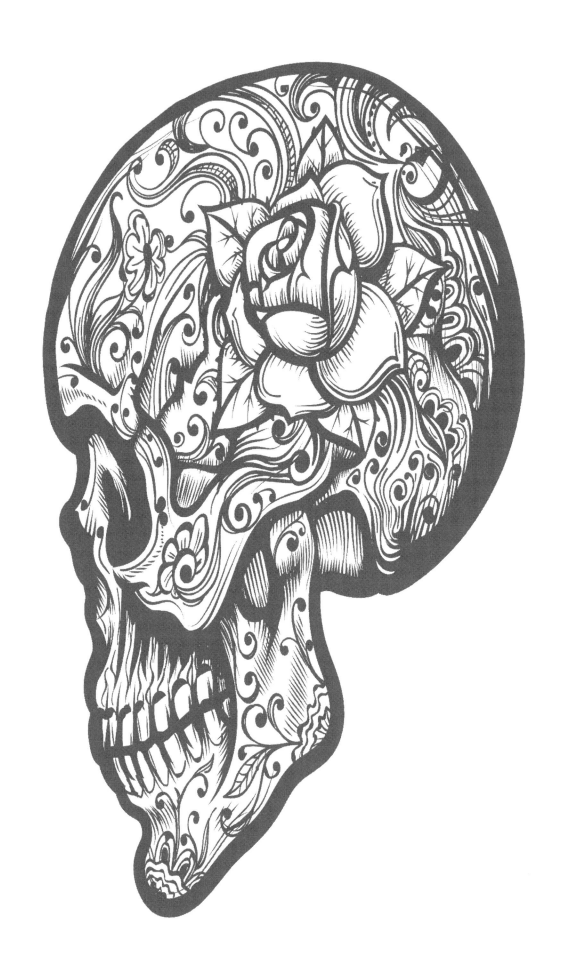

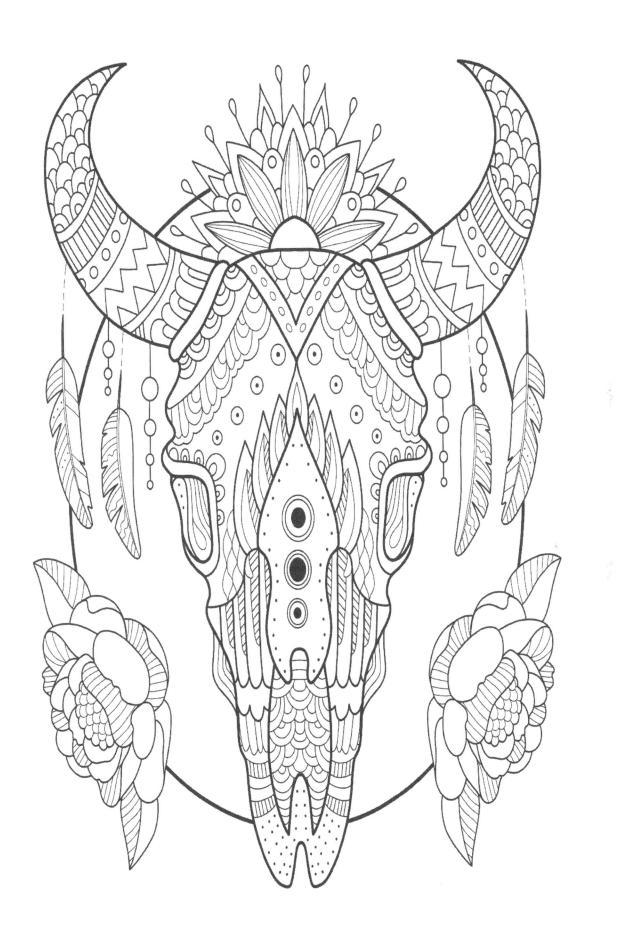

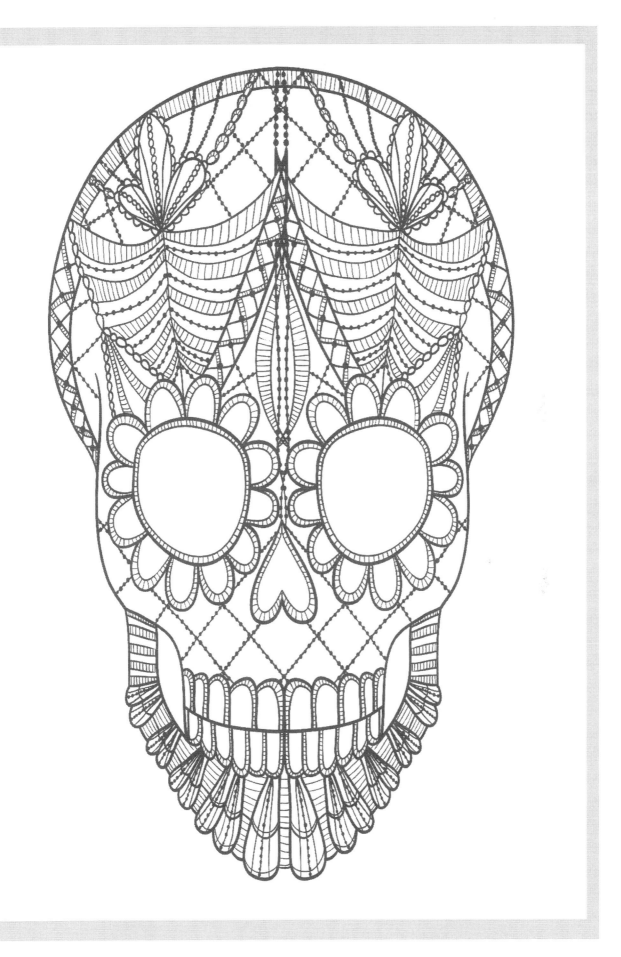

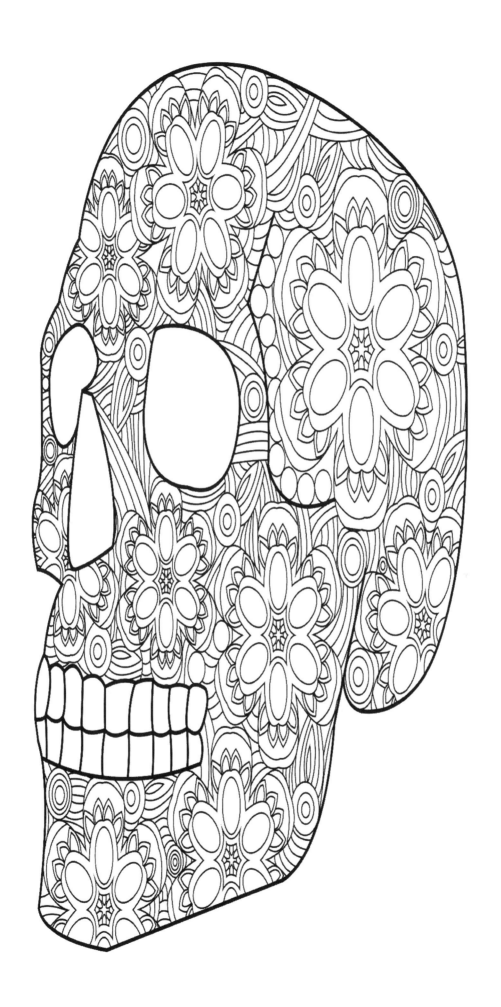

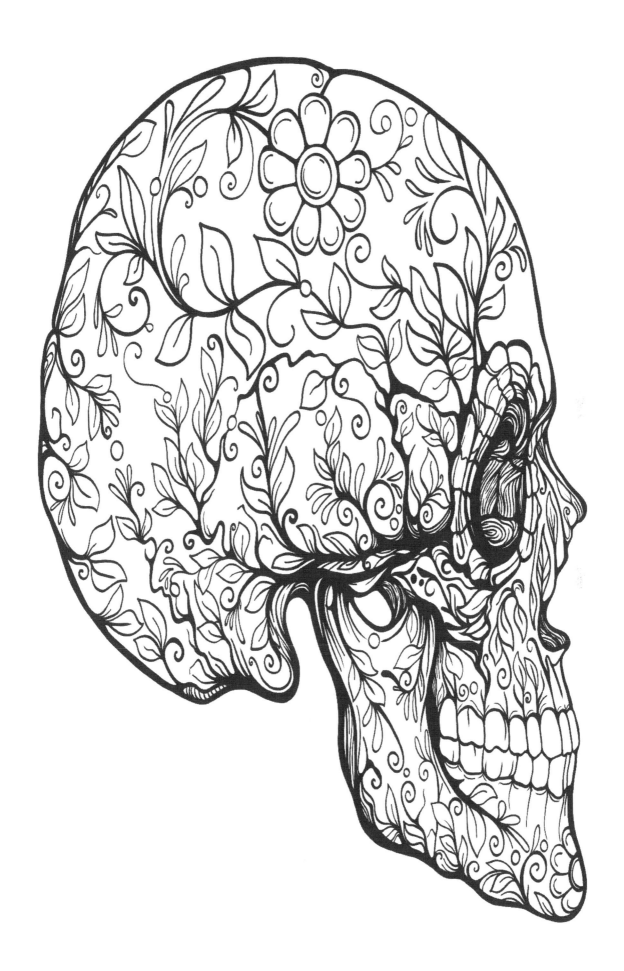

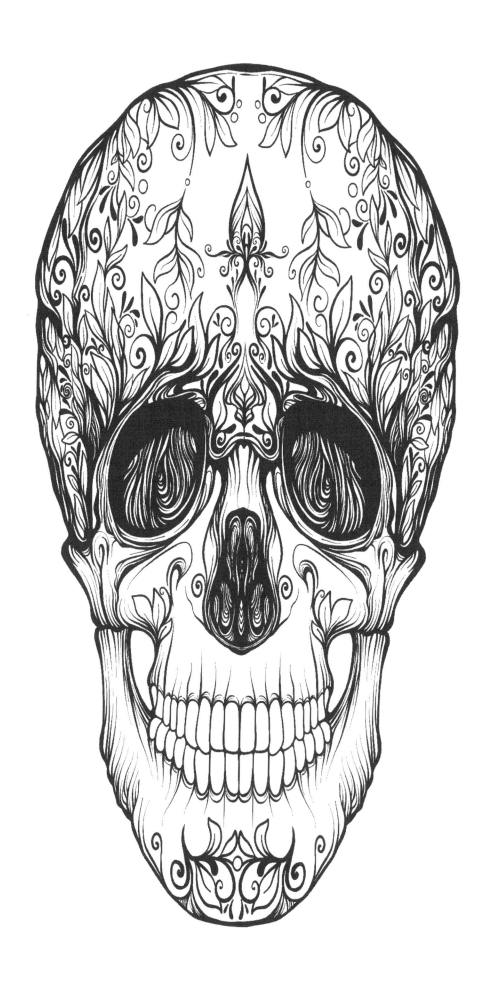

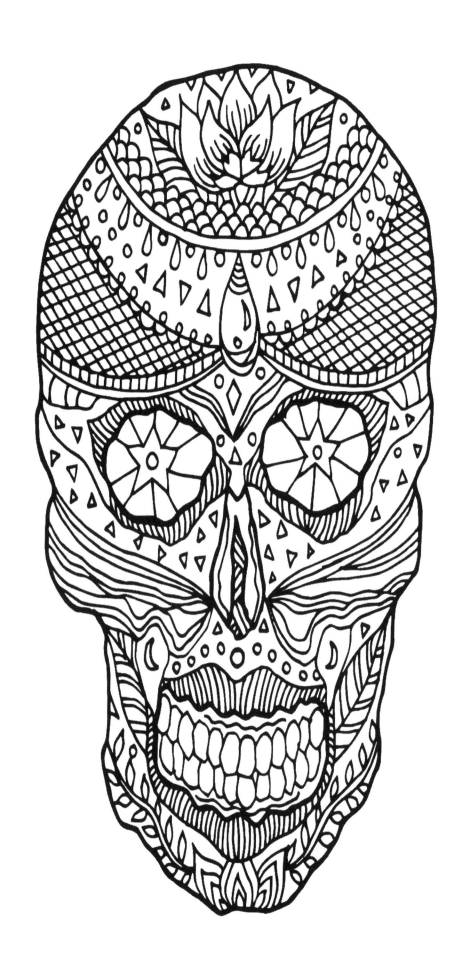

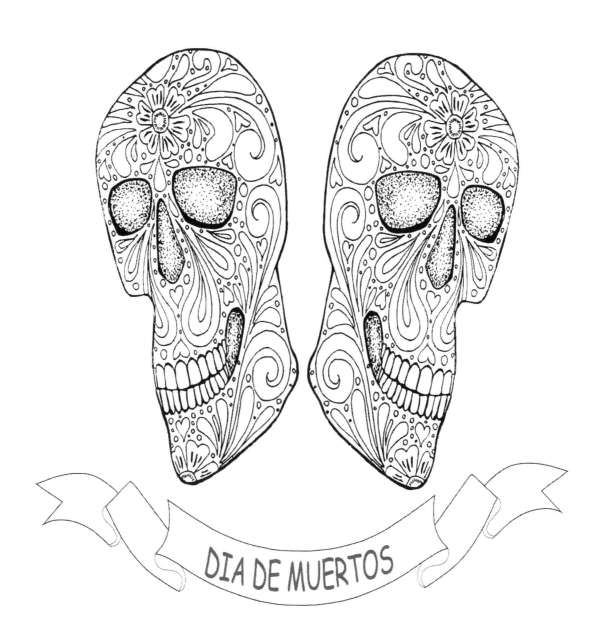

DIA DE MUERTOS

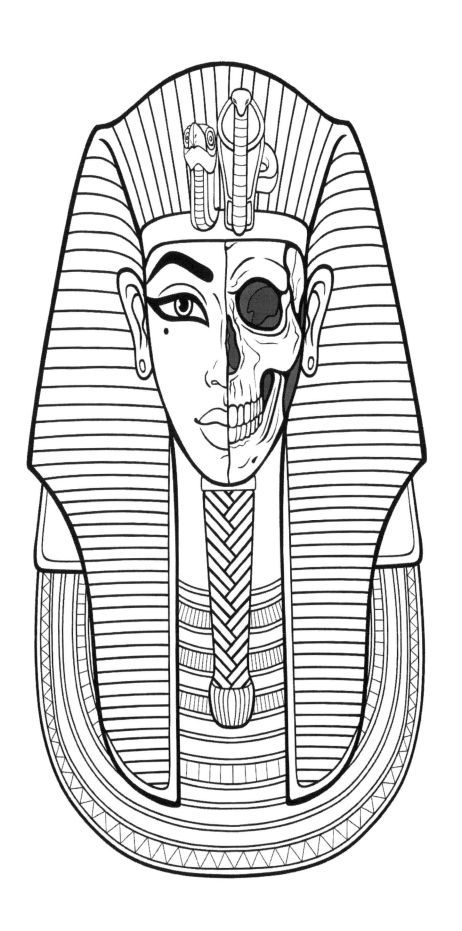

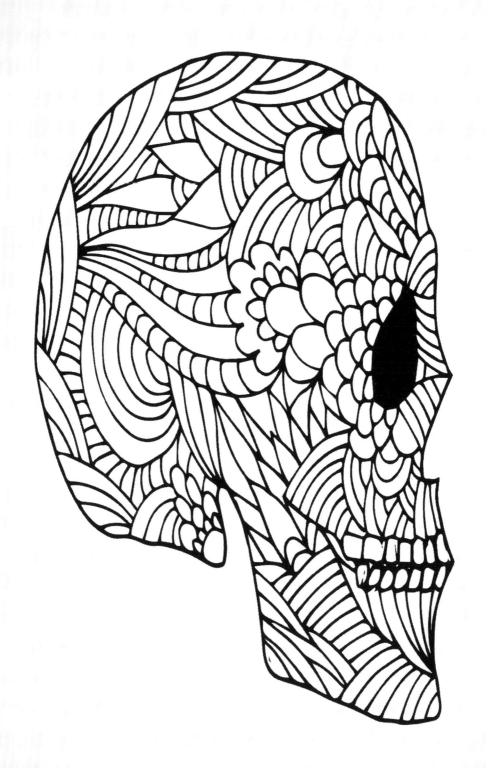

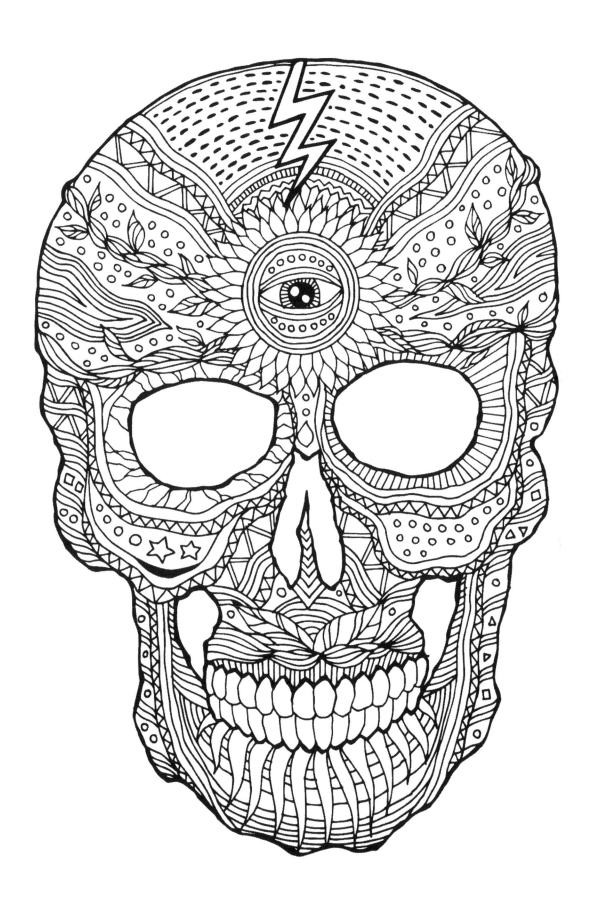

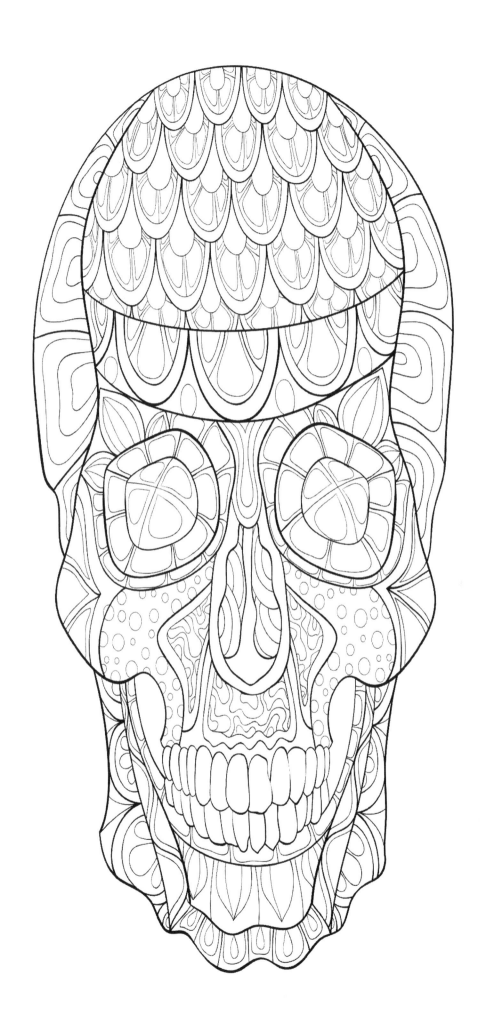

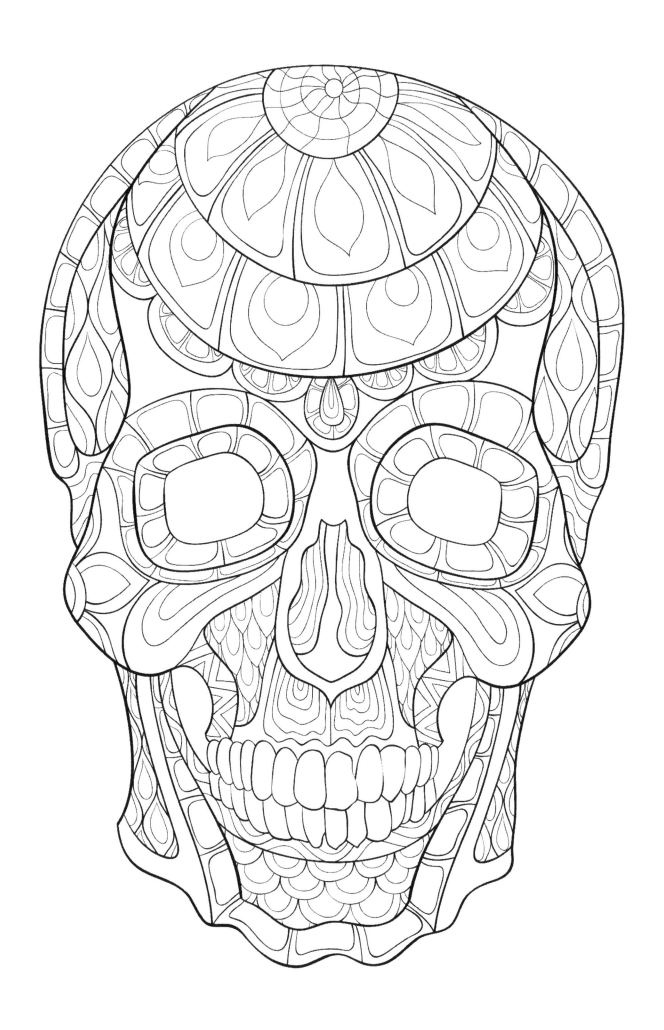

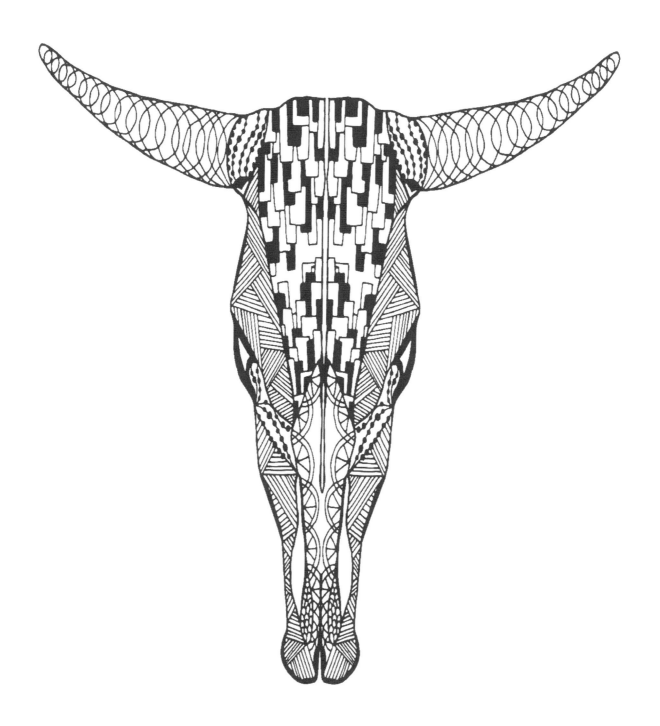

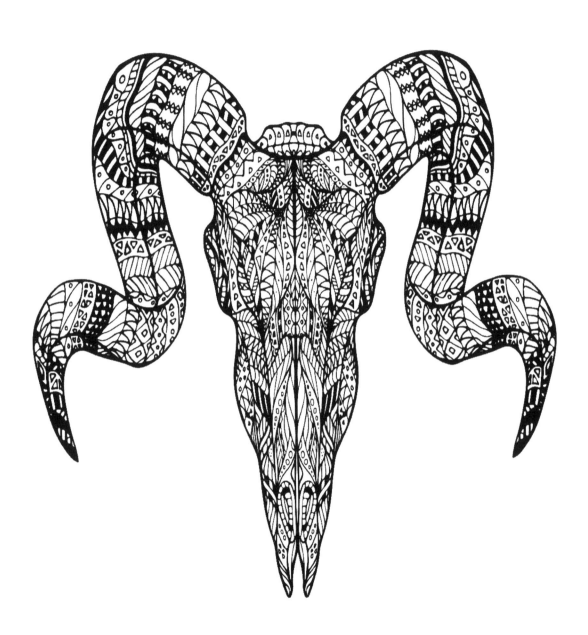

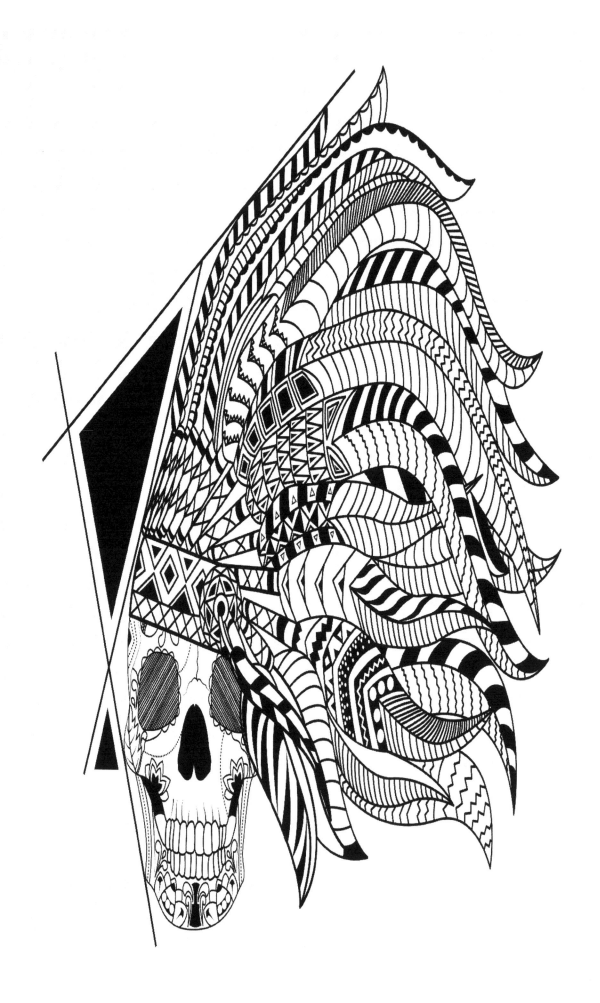

If you enjoyed this book, please leave me a review online.

About the author.

Dr. Wheeler is a physician by day and a writer by night. He is a retired Tae-kwon do instructor. He enjoys beekeeping, exercise, travel, gardening and family time. Be sure and collect his whole Fantastic Coloring Book series. Mandalas and More, Fantastic Animals, Fantastic Dogs, Fantastic Cats, Fantastic Horses, Fantastic Designs, and Fantastic Skulls.

He has plans for more coloring books on birds, dragons, flowers and more. For younger children look for The Adventures of Bumble the Bee in both coloring books and full color formats. The Boy Who thought he was a Horse and Fairy Tales a three book series. For fantasy lovers look up his two novels: Hammer of the Gods, The Nine Realms Book 1 and The Witch of Endor: Vampires, published by Novel Star. Poetry lovers will enjoy Dr. Wheeler's poems in Mystical Musings: A Collection of Poetry. He is currently working on Vampires: Love and Blood, the sequel to the Vampires saga.

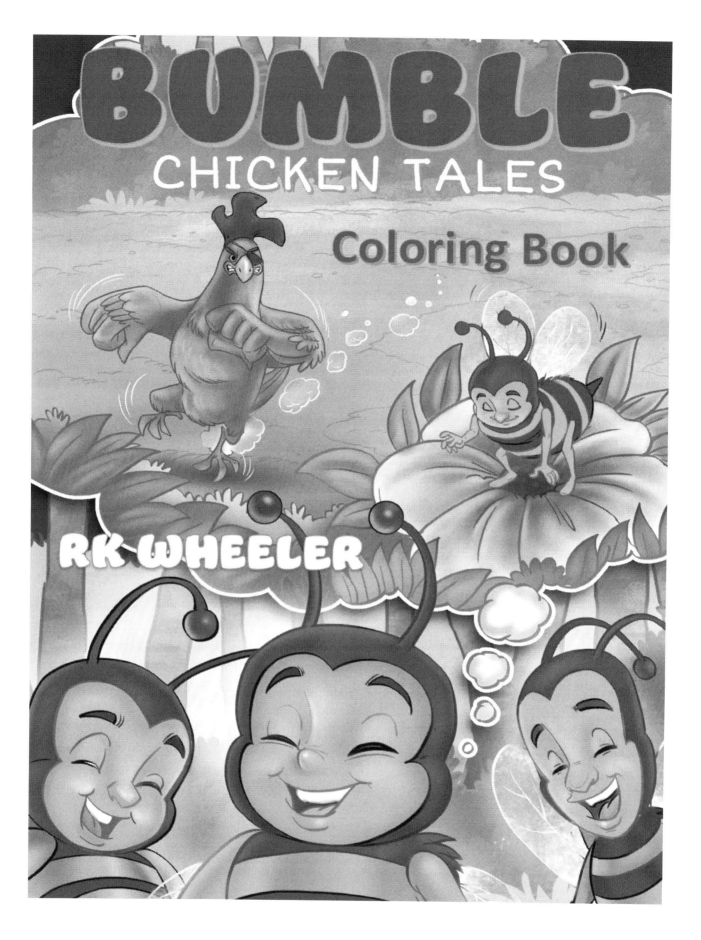

BUMBLE

The Bee Who Couldn't Fly

Coloring Book

By

B.K. Wheeler

The Witch
of Endor

VAMPIRES

R.K. Wheeler

RKWheeler.com

FANTASTIC ANIMALS

STRESS RELIEF

Dr. Robert K. WheelerJr.

100 Drawings

For Anxiety, Autism,

ADHD and

Depression

ADULT COLORING

BOOK

Made in the USA
Columbia, SC
18 March 2023

13584613R00061